Shi-shi-etko

Nicola I. Campbell

PICTURES BY
Kim LaFave

GROUNDWOOD BOOKS   HOUSE OF ANANSI PRESS   TORONTO   BERKELEY

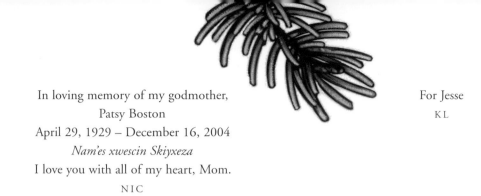

In loving memory of my godmother,
Patsy Boston
April 29, 1929 – December 16, 2004
Nam'es xwescin Skiyxeza
I love you with all of my heart, Mom.
N I C

For Jesse
K L

Acknowledgments
The author would like to thank the UBC First Nations House of Learning and
the UBC Department of Creative Writing.

Text copyright © 2005 by Nicola I. Campbell
Illustrations copyright © 2005 by Kim LaFave
Fourth printing 2009

Groundwood Books / House of Anansi Press
110 Spadina Avenue, Suite 801, Toronto, Ontario M5V 2K4
Distributed in the USA by Publishers Group West
1700 Fourth Street, Berkeley, CA 94710

ONTARIO ARTS COUNCIL
CONSEIL DES ARTS DE L'ONTARIO

We acknowledge for their financial support of our publishing program the Canada Council for the Arts, the Government of Canada through
the Book Publishing Industry Development Program (BPIDP) and the Ontario Arts Council.

Library and Archives Canada Cataloguing in Publication
Campbell, Nicola I.
Shi-shi-etko / Nicola I. Campbell ; pictures by Kim LaFave.
ISBN-13: 978-0-88899-659-6 ISBN-10: 0-88899-659-4
1. Native children–Canada–Juvenile fiction. 2. Indians of North America–Canada–Residential schools–Juvenile fiction.
I. LaFave, Kim II. Title.
PS8605.A5475S55 2004   jC813'.6   C2004-907268-4

The illustrations are digital.
Printed and bound in China

This story is about a little native girl named Shi-shi-etko, which means "she loves to play in the water." Shi-shi-etko's people have always lived in North America, hunting, fishing and gathering traditional foods and medicines, making their own clothing and building their own houses, making their own rules and taking care of their traditional territories, telling stories, singing and dancing. Native children were loved so much that the whole community raised them together – parents, grandparents, aunties, uncles, cousins and elders.

But now Shi-shi-etko has to go to Indian Residential School. It is the law. The school is far away from her home, and she will have to travel for a couple of days to get there. Once she arrives at school she won't see her parents for many months or even years, she will lose her traditional name, and she will be forced to speak English – a language she doesn't know.

For a long time the Canadian government believed that native people were uncivilized and made laws forcing native children as young as four, although generally between the ages of five and six, to go to residential school to learn European culture and religion. Parents were put in jail if they didn't send their children to these schools. Can you imagine a community without children? Can you imagine children without parents?

Residential schools had a huge impact on native people around the world, not only in Canada, but in the United States, Australia and New Zealand, as well. They resulted in a devastating loss of native traditions, languages and cultures. The last residential school in Canada closed in 1984.

The effects of the residential school system continue to hurt native people today. It is said that it will take seven generations for our people to heal.

Nicola I. Campbell

"One, two, three, four mornings left until I go to school,"
said Shi-shi-etko as she watched
sunlight dance butterfly steps
across her mother's sleeping face.

When streams of light
sent shadows across her mother's cheeks, she said,
"Mom, wake up. It's time for us to bathe
down by the creek."

Her mother blinked.
"You woke early today, Shi-shi-etko," she said,
swinging her feet to the floor.

With the first steps of sunrise
Shi-shi-etko skipped
along the worn path
through the cottonwood trees
all the way to the creek.

"My girl, we will not see each other
until the wild roses bloom in the spring
and the salmon have returned to our river.
I want you to remember the ways of our people.
I want you to remember our songs and our dances,
our laughter and our joy,
and I want you to remember our land."

Then her mother began to sing.
Her voice traveled from tree to tree,
flowing through the valley,
caught by the wind, carried
on the wings of eagles in flight.

Shi-shi-etko could not help herself.
She looked at everything —
tall grass swaying to the rhythm of the
breeze,
determined mosquitoes,
working bumblebees.
She memorized each shiny rock,
the sand beneath her feet,
crayfish and minnows and tadpoles
that squirmed between her toes,
all at the bottom of the creek.

They were almost home
when cousins, aunties and uncles
and the rhythmic tap of
Yayah's old cedar cane
could be heard through the trees.

"Mother! Father! They're here!"
Shi-shi-etko ran to greet her family.

Sunlight, wood smoke
and scents of barbecued
sockeye salmon
filled the air.
Dishes clattered,
footsteps pitter-pattered,
and laughter echoed from tree to tree.

Afterwards in the late-night silence,
tucked safely under Yayah's patchwork quilt,
Shi-shi-etko counted her fingers.
"There are only one, two, three more sleeps
until I go to school."

In the morning when Shi-shi-etko woke,
the sky was changing,
navy to brilliant blue.
She lay listening to the cool autumn breeze
sing morning songs.

Soft… drum… heart… beats.

"Let's take the canoe out on the lake," said her father.
Hand in hand they walked along the creek all the way to the lake.
"My girl, these are the things you must always remember," he said,
gesturing to the trees, mountains and water around them.
Together they picked up the canoe and carried it to the water's edge.

With yellow cedar paddles,
they strolled across smooth water.

Reach, dip, pull back…
Reach, dip, pull back…

The only sounds they heard
were the whistling birds
and their paddles breaking
the surface of the lake,
surrounding them with ripples.

Circle on… circle on… circle…

Her father sang the paddle song
that her grandfather used to sing.
His voice traveled across the water,
a chant that kept their pace.

Shi-shi-etko could not help herself.
She looked at everything.
She tasted the rain that fell on her face.
She listened as the water washed every rocky beach.
And when eagle song echoed through the valley,
traveling just beyond reach,
she sang her grandfather's paddle song,
and their voices echoed from beach to beach.

In a day full of sunlight,
Shi-shi-etko and her father returned
to pack her things.

Finally in the silence of night,
belly full, huddled safely under
Yayah's patchwork quilt,
Shi-shi-etko counted her fingers —
"One, two, only two more sleeps —"
then fell into
water-exhausted sleep.

Shi-shi-etko was dreaming
when she heard her yayah say,
"Shi-shi-etko, wake up, my girl.
We have some things to do today."

Yayah gave her a small bag
made from soft, tanned deer hide and sinew.
"This, my girl, is a bag for you to keep all your memories.
No matter where you go, no matter what you do,
remember to keep them safe."

The sun wasn't up yet
when they walked out the door and into the trees.
The path was dark and smelled alive
with rain, wet soil and leaves.
They walked until the sun was shining.

Yayah brought her to visit a great big fir tree.
Shi-shi-etko placed a sprig
into her bag of memories.
They visited a hemlock, a cedar,
even a pine, and each time
she placed a sprig
into her bag of memories.

They went to visit silver willow,
red willow, sage brush, cottonwood,
Labrador bushes and even kinnikinnick.
They visited blueberry, salmonberry,
saskatoon and huckleberry bushes.
They found bitterroot,
wild potato and wild celery patches.
On and on they went through fields of wild roses,
Indian paintbrush, fireweed and columbine.

Shi-shi-etko promised herself,
"I will remember everything."
Each plant they came to, she listened carefully to its name.
Then asked once, twice, even three times,
"Is it food or medicine, Yayah?
Is it always safe?"
Then, whispering its name,
she placed dried berry,
root, flower and fragrant leaf
into her bag of memories.

That night when Shi-shi-etko crawled
under her patchwork quilt,
she counted her fingers and said,
"One, only one more sleep."

At home the cattle truck
that gathered children waited.
Shi-shi-etko picked up her bag of memories,
a pinch of tobacco for offering,
then went out the back door
to her favorite place
beneath a great big fir tree.
She placed the tobacco at its base,
then tucked her bag inside its roots.

Dear Grandfather Tree,
Please keep my memories and my family safe.
I will be home in the spring.

"Shi-shi-etko, come inside now.
It's time for you to go."

When they rattled down
the dirt road and into the trees,
Shi-shi-etko held a sprig of fir
close to her heart.

Shi-shi-etko could not help herself.
She looked at everything —
tall grass swaying to the rhythm of the breeze,
determined mosquitoes,
working bumblebees.
She memorized each shiny rock,
the sand beneath her feet,
crayfish and minnows and tadpoles
that squirmed between her toes,
all at the bottom of the creek.